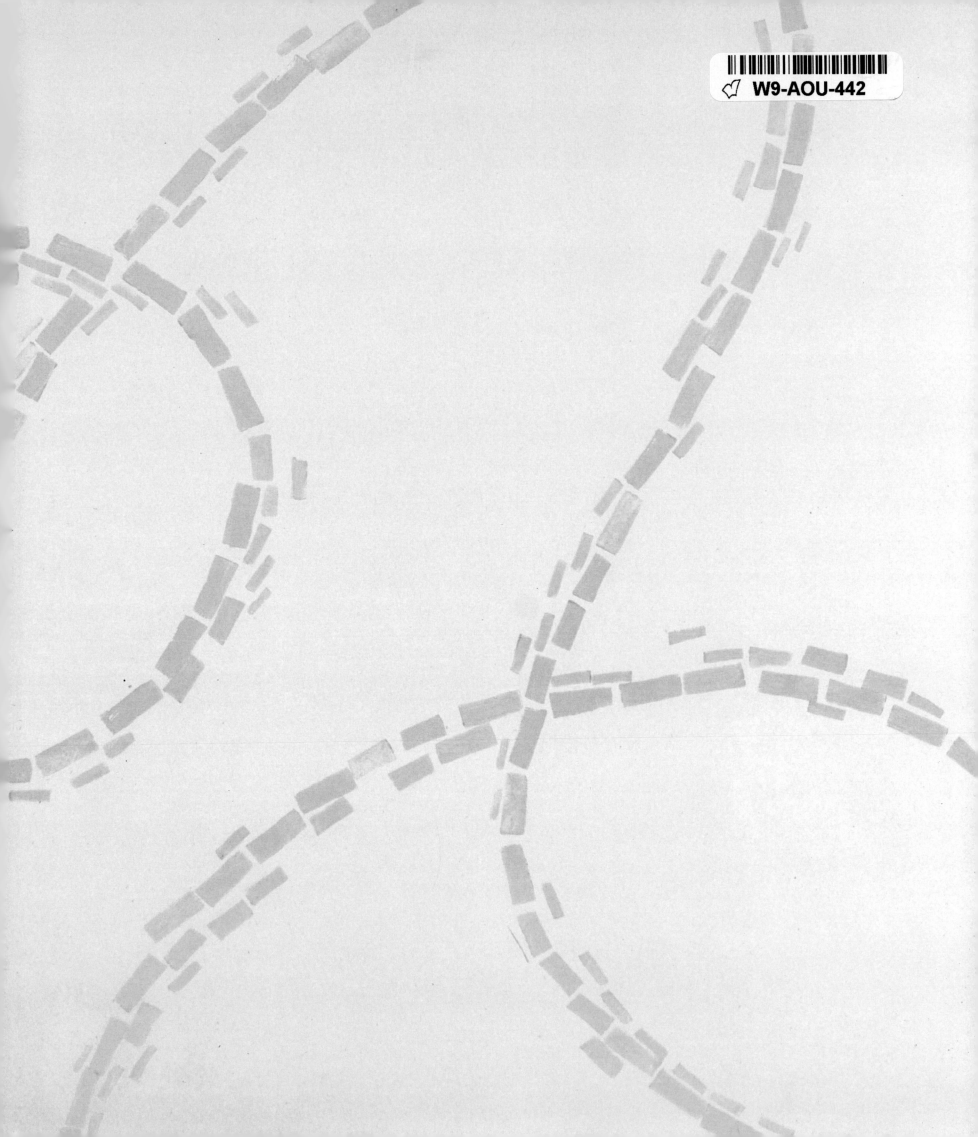

THE Wizard OF OZ

ADAPTED BY ANOUK FILIPPINI

FROM THE NOVEL BY L. FRANK BAUM

ILLUSTRATIONS BY ÉLODIE COUDRAY

AUZOU

Dorothy lived with her Uncle Henry and Aunt Em in Kansas, on a farm in the middle of nowhere. Whether you looked east, west, north, or south, the landscape was the same: scorched and barren prairies as far as the eyes could see.

Dorothy had just one friend and playmate, a little dog named Toto.

One day, a tornado swept over the prairie, lifted the house off the ground, and after a long journey, set it down in a far, far away land... all the way to the other side of the rainbow.

Cautiously, Dorothy and Toto stepped outside. They were welcomed by
a group of the strangest people who were only knee-high to a grasshopper
yet looked as old as the hills!

"Hooray! Congratulations, Dorothy! You have killed the Wicked Witch!" they sang.
"You must be mistaken," said Dorothy, apologetically. "I have not killed anyone."

Just then, a woman dressed in white appeared. She was very small,
very old, and very beautiful.

"When your house landed, it crushed the Wicked Witch of the East," she said.
"The Munchkins are very grateful to you because you have freed them from slavery."

"Are you the Queen of the Munchkins?" Dorothy asked.

"Me? No!" the woman replied. "I am the Good Witch of the North.
Take these silver shoes. They belonged to the Wicked Witch. They are yours, now."
  The shoes fitted perfectly.

  "I would like to go home and fine Aunt Em and Uncle Henry," Dorothy said.

    "I am sure they are worried. Can you help me?"

The Witch of the North frowned and thought hard.
"You must go to the Emerald City," she finally said. "The wonderful Wizard of Oz
lives there and he has more powers than the Witches of the East, West, South, and
North put together. I shall place a kiss on your forehead, which will protect you.
Go my child...You will find the Emerald City exactly in the center of the country."
With a wave of her hand, she pointed out a yellow brick road that meandered
endlessly into the distance.
"It's a long and dangerous journey, but my kiss will keep you safe from harm,"
she told Dorothy.

Dorothy took some food from the kitchen cupboard, closed the door and tucked the key into her pocket. She was ready to start on her journey. The sweet scent of flowers filled the air and birds were singing in the fruit-laden trees. The sun was shining brightly, yet it wasn't too hot. Much to her surprise, Dorothy felt somewhat carefree and joyful.

It was just then that she noticed the Scarecrow. He was waving his arms around madly, trying to catch her attention. Once Dorothy had unhooked him, he thanked her profusely while brushing down his thick woolen suit. Indeed, this Scarecrow had ears, eyes, and a mouth. So it could hear, see, and speak.

"Unfortunately, I have no brain," he told Dorothy. "If only I had one, I would be smart, like you."

"Come with me to the Emerald City to meet the Wizard of Oz," suggested Dorothy.

"If he can send me home, perhaps he can give you a brain."

They set off together on their journey into the heart of the Land of Oz. As they approached the edge of a glade, they heard someone groaning. Venturing into the forest, next to a cottage, Dorothy and the Scarecrow came across a strange, immobile man holding up an axe.

"I'm the Tin Woodman," he muttered between his teeth. "I got caught in the rain and my joints have rusted. I cannot move. Would you be kind enough to get my oil can?"

Once he was completely oiled, he invited them into his cottage and told them his story. A hundred years ago, he had fallen in love with the most beautiful girl in the region. But, the Wicked Witch of the East, who detested love, had changed him into a tin man.

"That's just awful!" exclaimed Dorothy.
"Not really, I just have to be careful not to rust. But I so wish I had a heart!
To love again..." he cried.
"Come with us to the Emerald City to meet the Wonderful Wizard of Oz,"
suggested Dorothy. "If he can send me home and give the Scarecrow a brain,
maybe he can give you a heart."

They were making their way through a dense forest when, all of a sudden, they heard a terrible roar, followed by a lion bounding out in front of them. The Tin Woodman and the Scarecrow were so terrified, they remained rooted to the spot.
Toto huddled up close to Dorothy, who furiously shouted at the lion, "You should be ashamed! Scaring a scarecrow, a tin man, a dog, and a little girl?" she screamed, "You are nothing but a coward to tackle anything smaller than yourself!"
"I know it" agreed the Lion, wiping away a tear with the tip of his tail. "Everyone is afraid of me, but I would so love to have some courage. After all, the king of the animals should have courage."
"Come with us to the Emerald City to meet the Wizard of Oz," suggested Dorothy in a softer voice. "If he can send me home, give the Scarecrow a brain, and the Tinman a heart, perhaps he can give you some courage."

They walked for days in a country populated by wild animals and filled with traps and hazards. Fortunately, Dorothy was protected by the kiss of the Witch of the North. And actually, they made a good team. One day, they were attacked by the Kalidahs: monsters with the body of a bear and the head of a tiger. They found themselves trapped on the edge of a deep ravine. However, the Scarecrow, who had no brain, came up with the idea of chopping down a large tree trunk to make a bridge. Next, the Cowardly Lion gathered up the little courage he had to carry his friends one by one on his back over the ravine. When they were all safe on the other side, the Tin Woodman cut down the tree trunk with his axe. The Kalidahs fell to their doom.

The Tin Woodman, who had no heart, quickly wiped a tear from his cheek before it made him rusty. He did not like to see living creatures die, even if they were really nasty.

That night, just like every night, they found shelter under
the trees and made a fire to keep warm.
"Who exactly is Oz?" asked Dorothy, after dining on a few walnuts.
"I have never seen him, but I have heard of him," replied the Cowardly Lion.
"Oz is a great magician and he can take on any form he likes. Some say
he looks like a bird, others an elephant, and others, a cat."
Dorothy sighed, lay down on a bed of leaves and soon fell asleep with Toto
in her arms. While the brainless Scarecrow, the Tin
Woodman without a heart and
the Cowardly Lion kept watch,
Dorothy dreamed
of the Wizard of Oz.

They finally reached the Emerald City where everything was green: the houses, the toys, and even the cotton candy! They were instructed to enter the wizard's throne room one at a time. When Dorothy entered, Oz had taken on the form of a head without a body, suspended in space above the throne.

When it was the Scarecrow's turn, Oz had turned into a beautiful young woman dressed in green silk.

"I, too, would love to have a pretty lady," said the Tin Woodman quietly.
"Pretty ladies understand matters of the heart."
However, he had to deal with a horrible, hairy monster.

Finally, the three friends pushed the Cowardly Lion into the throne room.
"It's your turn, now!" said Dorothy in a firm voice. "Be brave!"

To all, Oz the Great and Terrible asked why they sought him. And to all, Oz gave the same answer: he was willing to help them but first, they had to kill the WICKED, HORRIBLE, INFAMOUS Witch of the West, who ruled over the Winkie Country.

There was no road that led to the country of the Winkies because nobody ever went there. So, in order not to get lost, Dorothy and her friends had to follow the sun, which as everyone knows, sets in the west.
There was one good reason why nobody ever went to the Winkie Country: when the horrible witch saw travelers arriving from afar, she sent her faithful servants, the flying monkeys, to capture them. This is exactly what happened to Dorothy and her friends: the flying monkeys threw the Scarecrow, the Tin Woodman, and the Cowardly Lion into a cage. They then laid Dorothy very gently at the feet of the Witch of the West.

The Wicked Witch made Dorothy her slave. Separated from her friends, the young girl was desperate. How would they ever succeed in killing this horrible creature?

"There's no hope," she whispered. "I shall never go home."

One day, however, the Witch kicked Toto for absolutely no reason; simply out of spite. Dorothy was so angry she saw red. She grabbed the bucket of water she used to clean the floor and threw it over the Wicked Witch.

Miraculously, the Witch began to melt and eventually dissolved completely, like sugar in a cup of hot milk.

Dorothy was amazed. She had succeeded! Immediately, she ran to free her friends.

With the help of the flying monkeys, it only took them one day to return to the Emerald City. To their surprise, the throne room was empty, but suddenly a loud voice boomed out of nowhere.

"I am Oz, the Great and Terrible. What do you want?"

"Where are you?" asked Dorothy, surprised.

"I am everywhere and nowhere!" the voice answered.

Just then, Toto, who had been sniffing around the room, knocked down a large screen... and they couldn't believe their eyes! Right there in front of them stood a little pot-bellied man with a mustache who was busy operating a device with lots of handles. He was speaking into a big microphone, which made his voice echo loudly throughout the huge, vaulted room.

Dorothy stared at the little man in amazement. Was this really the Wizard of Oz? Had she and her friends come all this way and faced so many dangers for... nothing?

"Wait a minute!" she cried out. "Are you merely a charlatan?"

Oddly enough, the little man seemed very proud of himself. He puffed out his chest, blushed and replied, "Charlatan Oz at your service! Indeed, I am an impostor, but I'm the best there is. See for yourself."

He opened his large green cupboard and took out a variety of objects, which he used to make a heart for the Tin Woodman and a brain for the Scarecrow. As for the Cowardly Lion, the little man told him that he thought he was already very courageous but gave him, nevertheless, a herbal potion so he would never be afraid of anything again.
Only Dorothy was left disappointed. She realized that Oz had no solution for her. She would never go home.

Dorothy was wrong. Oz was perhaps an impostor, but he was extremely resourceful. Moreover, he was also longing to return home to America. With the help of all the inhabitants of the Emerald City, he made a huge hot-air balloon out of green patchwork fabrics. On the morning of their departure, the city gathered to say goodbye. But, just as the balloon was rising off the ground, Toto jumped out of the basket and disappeared into the crowd. Dorothy had no other choice but to jump out too.

"Find the Good Witch of the South!" shouted Oz. "She will know how to help you!"

The Good Witch of the South was sympathetic and kind.
She turned to Dorothy and said, "You do not know it, but your silver shoes are magical.
They have the power to take you wherever you want to go. Simply knock the heels
together three times. Go home and do not forget us."

Dorothy said goodbye to her friends, picked up Toto and clicked her heels three times.
She then found herself spinning through the air.
When she awoke, she was running with Toto along the path leading to Aunt Em and
Uncle Henry's farm. She stopped to catch her breath and saw that a rainbow had
formed in the cloudless sky. Dorothy gave a little wave. She was sure her friends up
there could see her. As she resumed her sprint toward the house, she thought to herself,
"there's no place like home."

General Director: Gauthier Auzou
Senior Editor: Maya Saenz-Arnaud
Layout: Alice Nominé, Eloïse Jensen
Production Manager: Jean-Christophe Collett
Production: Lucile Pierret
Project Management for the present edition: Ariane Laine-Forrest
Translation from French: Susan Allen Maurin
Proofreading: Rebecca Frazer
Original title: *Le Magicien d'Oz*

Printed in China, April 2016
ISBN : 978-2-7338-3924-9

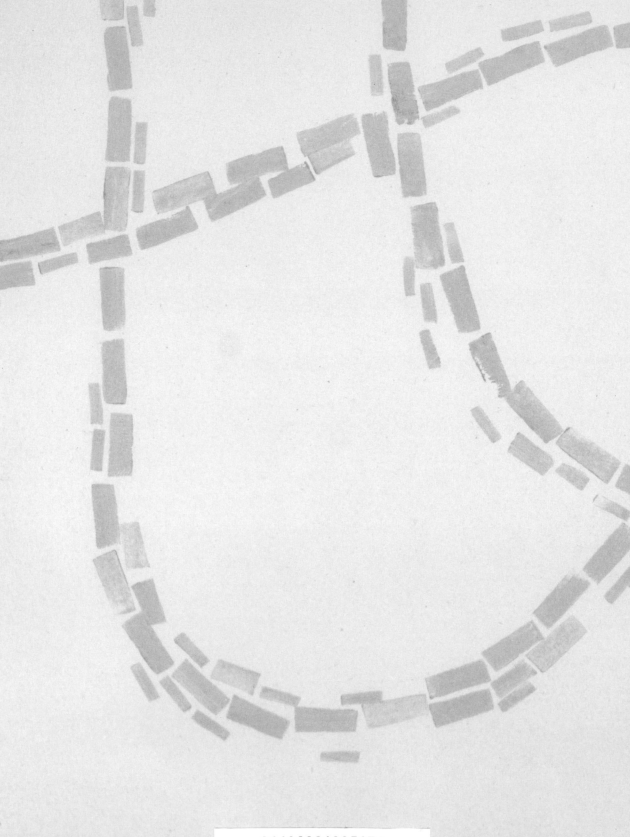